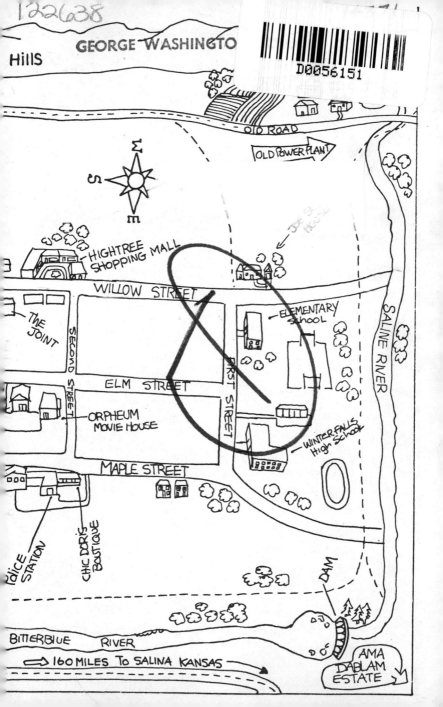

The Secret
of the
Invisible City

Jenny is bewildered by her "sweeping invitation" to a crystalline city called Krishna-la, where she meets aliens from a planet in a distant galaxy. They seem friendly enough, but their motives are unclear. Why did the aliens make it possible for Jenny and her friends to live out their most-dreamed about fantasies . . . and then why didn't the aliens protect Joe and Mike from attacks by Masai and samurai warriors? Nothing makes sense until Jenny finally unlocks the key to the puzzling SECRET OF THE INVISIBLE CITY.

THE JENNY DEAN SCIENCE FICTION
MYSTERY SERIES

The Secret
of the
Invisible City

By Dale Carlson

Illustrated by
Suzanne Richardson

Cover illustration by
Gino D'Achille

Publishers • GROSSET & DUNLAP • New York
A Division of The Putnam Publishing Group

For my daughter Hannah
who is my Jenny and my joy

ISBN: 0-448-19004-4
Library of Congress Card Catalog Number: 84-80178
Text copyright © 1984 by Dale Carlson.
Illustrations copyright © by Grosset & Dunlap.
All rights reserved.
Published simultaneously in Canada.
Printed in the United States of America.

Contents

CHAPTER 1

The Cyclone

"It's a cyclone!" cried Jenny Dean.

It was. A dark cloud of violently whirling winds in the shape of a funnel had suddenly appeared on the horizon of the bare Kansas plains. North and south winds of different temperatures had collided to create the terrifying storm that came twisting at forty miles an hour, destroying everything in its northeasterly path.

Jenny and three other Deans, her Aunt Sally, Uncle John, and cousin Martha, stood riveted outside the farmhouse. Normally, Aunt Sally, Uncle John, and cousin Martha lived in Kansas City. Normally, Jenny lived with her parents in Winter Falls, Kansas. On holidays—tomorrow was Thanksgiving—as many Deans as possible came to the old homestead, the farm out in the western plains of Kansas.

"But it's the wrong season for cyclones," said Jenny. "Cyclones happen in summer."

"You noticed," said Martha, teasing her cousin.

The cousins were glad to be together. Martha had been away during Jenny's last visit to Kansas City.

Jenny had such a well-developed capacity for noticing and remembering everything that her mother, the psychologist Dr. Gwen, her father Dr. Howard, the best veterinarian in Winter Falls, and Winter Falls' Detective Captain Ray Fisher often used Jenny's incredible capacities when they needed special observation work done. But people often teased Jenny, too, as her cousin Martha was now doing.

Only the four of them were going to need laughter before the day was out.

As much as Jenny Dean had a passion for the strange and bizarre, the coming of this oddly out-of-season cyclone heralded something more strange and more bizarre than anything Jenny had been involved with yet. It had been a season of strange cases! And she was supposed to be here on the family farm for a rest! Her special friend Mike Ward, her parents, and Captain Fisher had all insisted Jenny needed some peace and quiet.

"Some peace and quiet this is," said Jenny. She hugged Martha with affection. They were both sixteen, both juniors, both small, sturdy athletic girls with mops of short blond hair. The main difference was that Martha's eyes were a dreamy blue, and Jenny's were a bright, curious black, interested in everything on this planet and every other.

"Better get down into the cyclone cellar," said Uncle John, pulling gently on his pipe. Nothing ruffled Uncle John.

"Hurry, now," said Aunt Sally. "I'll get some food and blankets and shut the barn doors so the poor horses and cows don't panic. Then I'll see what I can do about the chickens. And, oh dear, where are Buster and Toni and Luscious?" The latter were Aunt Sally's cats, and Aunt Sally was off in a flurry to chase them down. Aunt Sally was as fluttery as Uncle John was calm. Uncle John was Dr. Howard's brother and the two were a lot alike.

"Jenny," cried Martha against the rising wind, "come inside. Aren't you coming, Jenny?"

"In a minute, Martha. It's so exciting out here," said Jenny

It was dangerous-looking. The dark cyclone twisted and careened in a path that would take it not too far from their own front door.

Jenny was amazed watching the dark, twisting storm covering hundreds of miles of vast, gray land and shooting high against the vast, gray sky. Nothing could take attention away from this cyclone. This part of Kansas was flat, thousands of flat miles of wheat and sorghum fields. The Arkansas River was miles away to the south. There was little wood, some cactus and yucca, and no more buffalo to plague the ranchers and farmers.

It was a bleak and lonely place.

"Fierce, isn't it?" said Uncle John.

"Fascinating, isn't it?" said Jenny. "Would it be too dangerous if I stayed out here, aboveground, Uncle John? I like watching that dark thing funnel its way across the plains."

"This storm's fierce, fascinating—and dangerous," said Uncle John. "It's out of season. It's an odd thing, it may change paths, no telling. Best come on down, Jenny," added Uncle John.

It was very dark now, and the wind howled. Jenny kept wondering what the calm at the cyclone's center was like, and whether there was anything caught up in there. She'd often wondered whether Dorothy was actually carried to Oz in that cyclone, or Oz had been carried in the cyclone's center to Kansas. These winds were powerful enough, whirling at two or three hundred miles an hour, with an updraft of a couple of hundred miles an hour, too. Why not? Anything could be in the eye of a storm like that.

"Jenny! Jenny Dean, you come down here right now," rose the nearly hysterical voice of Aunt Sally.

Martha wasn't waiting. She was small like Jenny and just as athletic. She darted out of the cyclone cellar door, grabbed Jenny's wrist, and pulled her down the cellar stairs. Uncle John closed the doors tightly after the girls.

They could hear the storm raging above them.

"Eat something," said Aunt Sally. "It'll take your minds off being afraid of that thing up there."

"Afraid?" said Martha, her mouth full of egg salad sandwich. "Look at Jenny. She's not afraid. The rest of us may be shaking. All she's doing is noticing every detail with her ears instead of her eyes, with her imagination instead of her fingers."

An hour passed before Uncle John opened the cellar doors to let them up. He felt it was such an unusual twister, he didn't want to risk any unusual trouble.

"May be the first twister in the history of Kansas to reverse its path," said Uncle John. "Your parents only made one of you, Jenny. They'd never forgive me if I didn't lock you away from the winds of a cyclone."

But the minute the doors were open, Jenny was out of the cellar. She raced for the stables. She wanted a horse to explore the cyclone's path, to see its effects, to see what it left behind.

"Coming, Martha?" Jenny paused just long enough to invite her cousin.

"Another time," Martha said as sweetly as she could, not wanting to suggest her feeling Jenny was as crazy as a March Hare to go out there. "A bubble bath sounds better to me."

"Right," said Jenny as sweetly as she could, not wanting to suggest her feeling Martha was crazy for not wanting to explore the path of a cyclone as fierce as this.

She saddled up the roan mare and took off across the fields in the direction she had last seen the dark shape of the funneling winds.

She rode for several miles before she came across the path of destruction. And destruction was what she found. The descriptions she had read of cyclones were all too true. Trees had been uprooted. Barns had shattered to the ground, their pieces flung everywhere. Silos had been smashed. Farm equipment, even heavy tractors had been thrown sideways for hundreds of feet.

Jenny kept riding. She rode miles away, across wheat fields and then across just bare, empty plains, following the clear trail southwest from where the cyclone came barreling northeast.

In the middle of nothing, the mare suddenly balked.

"Come on, sweetheart, there's a good girl," cooed Jenny.

But 'sweetheart, there's a good girl,' didn't get the mare to move. Jenny climbed down to lead her a little way. Nothing doing. Jenny ran ahead at a canter, hoping the roan would follow.

Not only didn't the roan follow, but something unbelievable happened to Jenny. Running at a pretty fast clip, she slammed her forehead against something hard. She was thrown backward by the impact. Her bones rang sharply as she hit the earth.

"It's impossible, Jenny," Jenny said out loud to herself. "Jenny," she repeated to herself, "it's impossible."

In the middle of nowhere, with nothing visible in front of her, to the side of her, or behind her, Jenny had run hard into a thoroughly solid—and completely *invisible*—wall. The cyclone had left something behind in its path, all right.

But what?

CHAPTER 2

Blackout

"Isn't this marvelous?" Jenny said out loud to no one in particular.

She had stood up instantly and brushed herself off. She was now trying to feel the shape, the height, anything at all of this invisible shield.

"Well, what do you think?" Jenny now addressed the roan mare. "Is it a solid barrier, some sort of see-through plastic I never heard of before? There's no distortion when you look through it, like when you look through Lucite or Saran Wrap. Or is it not material at all? Is it a force field of some kind, like an electro-magnetic or gravitational field? I mean, you can't see an electro-magnetic field or a gravitational field—you can only know they're there because of the effects they have on things."

Jenny sighed at the horse. "It's all right. I babble when I get nervous."

She had been feeling the invisible wall for fifteen

minutes. She couldn't reach the top, so it had to be higher than six feet tall. She hadn't found any beginning or end, so it was longer than half a mile, which was how far Jenny walked at this particular pace in fifteen minutes.

The mare had followed Jenny at a safe distance. The horse's occasional snort, her nervous gamboling and earth-pawing indicated to Jenny that there was something around here that even the horse found unusual.

Jenny's curiosity, however, had always outlasted her fear. She didn't want to go back to the farm without finding out something, anything. Jenny continued to feel and poke the invisible force field, or shield, or whatever it was. Finally, she felt something, all right.

She felt an electric shock. Then suddenly, she had a premonition she was about to black out—and did.

The next thing Jenny knew, she was no longer exploring force fields in the middle of an endless nowhere in the aftermath of a dark cyclone. She was lying in her bed, in her room at the farmhouse. Morning sunlight was streaming across her patchwork quilt. Aunt Sally, Uncle John with his pipe, and Martha, wringing her hands, were hovering at the foot of her brass bed.

"Well?" said Martha. "We thought you some-how managed to get tornadoed away, chasing the cyclone's path like that. I only have one cousin, you know."

"Cranky, isn't she?" said Jenny sweetly. "How did I get here? The last thing I remember was being thrown by some kind of electrical current—"

"I don't know about any electrical currents," said Aunt Sally. "We found you wandering around in a daze with the roan, on the other side of the silo, after dinner last night. We all had been out looking for you."

"Sorry, Aunt Sally," said Jenny. She realized her aunt and uncle weren't used to her sudden exploratory disappearances the way her own parents were. And there weren't any street-corner phones out on the plains to check in from. "Really, I am."

"Well," said Uncle John. "Long as you're safe."

Aunt Sally rounded the brass knobs at the foot of the bed to give Jenny a quick, forgiving hug. "Breakfast in ten minutes," she said. "You've certainly had enough sleep, ten hours' worth, any-way."

"Wonderful dreams, too," murmured Jenny, "wonderful dreams about a city of crystal palaces and several beautiful, royal people, and—what are these blue marks on my wrists?''

Jenny suddenly noticed two round, blue marks on top of and underneath her wrists. They were painless, so obviously they weren't bruises.

''We wondered, too,'' said Martha, plunking down near Jenny on the patchwork quilt.

Aunt Sally, who was interested in fixing stacks of wheatcakes and heating syrup and checking on what was in the oven for Thanksgiving dinner, left the two small, blond cousins to their own energetic inquiries.

''I wonder if the blue marks and the electric shock and the crystal palaces and those beautiful people have any connection,'' said Jenny.

Her bright, dark eyes were alight with the possibility of an interesting quest. Her passion in life, besides the psychology of human experience (Jenny wanted to be a psychologist like her mother) and animals (she adored them like her father, and often played her guitar to soothe them), was old movies, especially those with bizarre and dangerous plots.

''It's Thanksgiving,'' Martha begged, seeing an old and familiar gleam in her cousin's eyes. ''Couldn't we just eat food instead of doing living reels of *Jenny Treks Kansas Plains in Search of An Outer Space Frankenstein*?''

"Martha!" Jenny cried, leaping out from under the patchwork quilt. "Martha, you may have got it!"

"Got what?" said Martha. Then she held up her hand like a stop sign. "No, don't tell me. I don't want to know anything but how much food I can put in my face until sundown."

There was no time for explanations anyway. The telephone rang throughout the old farmhouse. It was a long-distance call from Winter Falls for Jenny.

"Hi, darling, Happy Thanksgiving," came Dr. Gwen's voice over the phone. "I miss you. Wish we could be there, but what with my two new patients and your dad's sudden rash of cows everywhere with some sort of bovine intestinal flu, I'm afraid we're stuck up here for the whole holiday."

"I miss you, too," said Jenny. She meant it. She and her mother not only looked alike and sounded alike, but thought so much alike they often didn't even have to talk. It was this psychic closeness Jenny truly missed when they were apart.

Dr. Howard said hello to his daughter, too, then put Mike Ward on the line. Mike and Jenny had been friends since the second grade. Last year something more special had happened between them, and now Jenny was Mike's girl as well as his friend. Since Mike wanted to be a Dr. Howard-kind of veterinarian as Jenny wanted to be a Dr. Gwen-kind of psychologist, they both hoped to have a home like the Deans someday, where people and animals came when they hurt and left when they felt better. But that was someday.

Right now, there was a lot of living they enjoyed together. They were both athletes, tennis players for the Winter Falls High School team, both scientists by nature, and both shared a passion for the weird. The way Jenny liked old movies, Mike liked mystery stories. They spent a lot of time together exploring the unknown, sometimes on their own, sometimes in the service of Detective Captain Ray Fisher.

"Laurie and Joe send their love and I send mine," said Mike, after he and Jenny exchanged news. Laurie Harper and Joe Scott were their closest friends at Winter Falls High.

"Send mine back, but keep most of mine for yourself," said Jenny. "Bye, everyone. See you soon."

"You didn't say a word about the cyclone or whatever it was that happened to you," said Martha.

"They'd worry," said Jenny.

"The way you are, I can see why," said Martha.

After breakfast, everyone helped Aunt Sally dust,

clean, and straighten the sprawling farmhouse. There were only three other farms within a two-hour automobile ride this side of the Arkansas River, and two of the three families were coming for Aunt Sally's three-o'clock Thanksgiving feast.

"I wish your friend Captain Fisher had accepted our invitation," said Uncle John. "Sounds like an interesting man. I'd have liked meeting him."

"He is an interesting man," said Jenny. "He's also, along with my dad, the strongest, smartest grown man I know—and a complete vegetarian. He says everyone who doesn't eat one more creature, means one less creature will be killed. So he doesn't go to people's houses at holiday time, his feelings, he says, being his own. I must admit, though, my dad and I are beginning to share Captain Fisher's feelings."

"Well, not today, I hope," said Aunt Sally. "There's so much here to eat."

What Aunt Sally had made, as usual, for Thanksgiving dinner, was everything. There were all the usual vegetables and sweet potatoes and apple and cherry pies and home-baked bread and popovers and home-preserved jellies and jams and pickles and relish, and two enormous stuffed turkeys.

Jenny and Martha and Uncle John carried serving

dishes around and set the table and tripped over each other doing kitchen duty.

"You girls have been such a help," said Aunt Sally, "you're excused for a while. Uncle John will help me do the rest of the setting up. You two go out and get some fresh air for a while before dinner."

"Oops," said Martha, "too late. Company's coming."

The girls had to postpone their ramble until thirteen people had eaten enough for thirty-three.

"How about now, Aunt Sally?" Jenny asked. "Can Martha and I go saddle up and ramble for an hour to work off all this food? I promise we'll do the dishes later."

Permission was granted.

An hour later, however, only Martha was back.

"Where's Jenny, dear?" said Aunt Sally.

"I know you're going to find this hard to believe," said Martha, "but I've lost her. We were riding out in the middle of nowhere, and suddenly, Jenny was gone."

CHAPTER 3

Behind the Force Field

"I'm gone, all right," said Jenny. "At least my mind is. Nothing so beautiful could really exist."

Horseless and still tingling from another slight electric shock—Jenny had somehow been pulled through the force field. She found herself at the beginning of a narrow street that wound through the most incredible city she had ever seen.

"It isn't possible," she said.

Before her rose a small city so delicate, so airy, that it seemed to float in the sunlight between earth and sky. Its buildings were made of a material like rock crystal or a transparent quartz. Domed towers, spires, windows and balconies with latticework like glass lace decorated every small home and shop along the streets. Then Jenny saw an exquisite collection of towers and minarets high above the rest, gleaming against the clouds. That must be a great palace, Jenny thought.

29

The crystalline buildings were so white, gleaming like perfect blue diamonds in the brilliant sunlight.

"Welcome to Krishna-la, in your Earth language, Valley of the Blue Stars, I believe," said a deep voice, startlingly close, considering Jenny had seen no one about in the street she was wandering through.

And for some reason beyond Jenny's knowledge of physics, though one ought to be able to see through buildings made of clear crystal, she couldn't. So if there were people inside the buildings, Jenny hadn't been able to see or hear any of them.

"I am Allessi," said the deep, pleasant voice.

Its owner stood before Jenny, all of a sudden and all bathed in light so Jenny could hardly get much of a look at him.

She had by now progressed up the street to what was a pretty garden, with small, flowering trees, bushes in bloom, and brightly colored birds with big, fanning tails like peacocks.

Among the peacocks, another figure appeared. "And I'm Allessa," said a voice like tinkling glass.

"And we are Dora, Mara, and Damon Lanza," said three more voices, "children to Allessi and Allessa—did we get that right?"

English was not, then, Jenny decided, their native

BEHIND THE FORCE FIELD 31

language. Not surprising. But what could surprise her at this point?

"Will you speak?" said Allessi, kindly.

"It's possible she can't see us and that makes her nervous," suggested Allessa. "Do you remember in the computer room yesterday, when we examined the human eye of her? Or is the grammar just *her* human eye? Anyway, whichever the English is, it turned out that the human eye of Earth has trouble with very bright light. I mean, Earth people only have two lids, after all."

Jenny glanced down at the blue marks on her wrists, feeling instantly she had understood Allessa accurately. During that blackout, when Jenny couldn't remember where she'd been or what had happened, she had come through the force field as she had today. She had been taken for an examination, and then returned to the Kansas plains with no memory of the City of Krishna-la, the examination or anything.

"True," said a young man's voice. It had to be Damon Lanza, and he had to have read her mind.

"Yes, we're telepaths. You can be, too, if you like," said Damon Lanza cheerfully.

"We're sorry about the blue marks, Jenny," said Allessa, "but we hadn't studied the texture of human skin yet. The marks will disappear soon.

They won't appear again. But what about the light, Allessi?''

''We'll make Jenny a pair of splendid sunglasses this evening,'' said Allessi. ''Until then, she'll be able to see better indoors. The sun on what Earth people call crystal is very wearing on their optic nerves. Will you come with us up to the Palace of the Winds for—supper? Wouldn't it be supper at about this time on Earth?''

Allessi continued as they walked. ''We are Allessi and Allessa this term, Heads of State just now, and so we live up at the palace. But the Heads of State in Krishna-la are rotated constantly, thank goodness. Soon it will be someone else's turn to chair the meetings and make the coffee and clean two or three hundred crystal rooms. In Krishna-la, our Heads of State have no authority, you know. We are more like trusted housekeepers of the Palace of the Winds.''

They had, all six, continued to walk as they talked. Soon they had come through the arch and across the crystal-cobbled courtyard and entered the vast, shining rooms of the palace.

Allessa was right. When Jenny's eyes were shaded from the glitter of direct sunlight careening like diamonds from everything in sight, she was

finally able to see the shapes and forms and faces of her hosts.

They were all tall and lovely and dark-haired. All five were dressed simply, in white India cotton tunic shirts and full trousers. The five, Allessi, Allessa, Dora, Mara, and Damon Lanza, were so remarkably similar, Jenny thought, it was almost as if they had drawn the same issue body type along with their clothes.

What an odd idea to have, Jenny thought. I wonder what put that into my head.

"Quite right, too," said Allessi.

There was a large, round table in the center of the main palace hall. The table and chairs looked as if they had been carved out of ice. They were warm enough to the touch, though. Possibly a form of plexiglass, thought Jenny, as they all sat down to tea and quite ordinary lettuce-and-tomato sandwiches and carrot cake.

"Quite right again," said Allessi. "Yes, this is a form of plexiglass. And yes, all Krishna-lanians possess the power of cellular metamorphosis. It simply means we can change our cells and bodily forms to look any way we choose."

Jenny blinked at the scientific impact of such a power.

That also means you could regenerate. If a leg or arm or eye were broken or damaged or removed, you could grow new ones, she thought.

"Quite right once more," said Allessi.

"Oh my," said Jenny. "Oh my."

It was a short phrase any of Jenny's family and close friends would have recognized. It signified that even Jenny Dean the chatty had lost her tongue in sheer amazement.

Might as well plunge right into it now, before I get lost in the details, Jenny decided. This time, though, she spoke aloud instead of waiting to have her mind read.

"This is going to sound idiotic," said Jenny, "but you don't exactly come from around here, do you?"

Allessa's voice sounded again like musical tinkling glass. "No, not exactly from around here. Actually, we come from the Andromeda Galaxy. It's the sister galaxy to your own Milky Way."

"Slowly, please," said Jenny. "This, how shall I say, boggles an Earth mind, since we can't even travel at the speed of light yet, and therefore couldn't begin to think of space travel as you're describing it. I mean, we can't even get four light-years away to our nearest star, much less out of our own galaxy, much less half a million parsecs to the next galaxy.''

"That's because you're still depending on machinery power instead of mental power, although we have a good energy transformer that can transport bodies long distances very quickly,'' said Damon Lanza. "The transformer simply disintegrates your particles and reassembles them somewhere else.''

Jenny's instinct, just hearing about that, was to hug herself, hold herself together.

The two younger girls laughed. Jenny judged Damon Lanza to be about her own age, Dora and Mara about twelve and thirteen.

"May I ask something that is probably simpleminded to you, but mind-blowing to me?'' said Jenny. "Is Krishna-la a starship? A space city? Is it solid, or a projected image from far away? Or is this all just a dream I'm having?'' she couldn't help adding wryly.

The blue marks on her wrists were real enough for the moment to persuade Jenny to go on inquiring.

"I mean, we're beginning to build models in our own laboratories on Earth for future space settlements, but they don't look like this,'' said Jenny.

"Ours look more like globes and doughnuts and beaded necklaces. Krishna-la is so beautiful."

"Thank you," answered Allessi. "All we've done is learn how easy it is to throw a kind of crystal bubble around any of our smaller cities. We use blocks of another sort of fissionable crystal for propulsion energy and power aboard our star city. And then, just as you on Earth would say, we take off."

"But the distances are incredible," said Jenny. "How did you manage to get here alive?"

"We travel faster than the speed of light," said Damon Lanza. "When we have to, we travel in a time warp. And so we stay, actually, exactly the same age as long as we're in space. I'm myself still only about two thousand years old."

Damon Lanza looked about Jenny's age.

"What's life expectancy on your planet?" said Jenny. Travel across the vastness of space *would* be easier for a longer-lived people than humans.

"About ten thousand years," said Damon Lanza.

Jenny did some quick equations. "Right," she said. "If you lived on Earth you would be about sixteen."

Jenny kept looking at how alike they looked and how beautiful they were. "May I ask, do you, when you're on your planet, look as you do now?" It was the question she had wanted to ask earlier, but it had seemed too personal at first.

Now all questions seemed just an interesting matter of scientific information the Krishna-la people were delighted to share.

Allessa and her two daughters burst into laughter. Allessi gave them a reproving look.

"We're sorry, my dear," said the silvery voice of Allessa. "It's just that Earth bodies seem a bit impractical. We're wearing them so we won't frighten any Earth people we happen to invite behind our force field. We don't want to appear too strange to you. But you'll admit, Jenny, your mind is so quick that to have only two eyes, ears, arms and other things seems a bit—how shall I say it, impoverished?"

"Okay, I'll ask," said Jenny, nervously. "How many arms and things do your bodies normally have in Krishna-la?"

"Several," said Allessa promptly. "And we grow more as needed."

Jenny warded off the idea straight-armed, the way Martha did when she didn't want to see or know something.

"Don't show me," said Jenny. "I'm having enough trouble getting all this as it is. I do have two more questions for now, and then I think my head needs a rest.''

"Ask all you want," said Allessi. "It's only fair after last evening. That's when we wired you into *our* computer library and taped human Earth history, biology, and all kinds of other information from your mind.''

"First," said Jenny. "How come we can't see you or your city in the middle of Kansas?''

"Our landing did seem to stir up your atmosphere, didn't it?'' said Allessi.

"Yes, an out-of-season cyclone appeared," said Jenny. "But then—nothing.''

"Millennia ago, we conquered the violence in ourselves. We do not kill except under extreme or extraordinary circumstances. But on many of the planets we visit, we still find creatures such as yourselves on Earth who are still so dangerous to themselves and others. What we invented to defend ourselves are simple image deflectors. Wherever we are, we can deflect our image with a sort of mirror, you would call it, to make our image establish itself elsewhere. It's a bit like bending light rays. Right now, for instance, the image of Krishna-la is not far from Alpha Centauri, the nearest star system to Earth you mentioned a while ago.''

"Amazing," said Jenny, grasping the purpose of this. "No one can see you so you can't be shot at."

"Exactly," said Allessi. "We have large civic image deflectors to hide a whole star city. And when visiting strange places, each of us carries a small one. If trouble comes, we can simply *look* as if we're somewhere else."

"That's some defense mechanism," said Jenny. "Captain Fisher would like that. It's so absolutely nonviolent."

"And your second question?" said Allessi.

"Since you've studied my mind, you'll have found out that most Earth people, me included, are nervous, suspicious, and easily alarmed at the unknown," said Jenny, as smoothly as a small, grow ing panic inside her would allow. "Therefore, as beautiful as I find you and your Valley of the Blue Stars, and as much as I thank you for our exchange of interesting information—"

Jenny suddenly couldn't stand being in this alien place one more minute, without knowing if she were free or a prisoner.

The words came out in a rush. "What I want to know is—how long are you going to keep me here?"

As she heard her own voice, it sounded like the forlorn wailing of the prairie wind.

CHAPTER 4

Back in Kansas

As if in answer to Jenny's question, she had the now familiar sensation of being about to black out. Then she did black out.

She was back in Kansas, just outside the farmhouse. As Allessa had promised, the blue marks had disappeared from her wrists. Now Jenny had red marks on her knees. But those were from kneeling on the hard, winter soil in Aunt Sally's herb garden. Jenny seemed to have been cutting back the oregano, considering the garden scissors in her hand and the pile of dried stalks by her side in the dying grass.

"Okay," said Jenny, opening a discussion with herself. "I have several options here. I could have made up the entire thing. Somebody could have hypnotized me into believing the entire thing. Or it's all entirely real."

41

"Sorry to have worried you, Mom. She's out here," Martha called, looking out the kitchen window over Jenny's head and hollering back to Aunt Sally. "She must have wandered away from me somehow and come back another way."

Martha's voice addressed Jenny more quietly. "Where were you? I was scared to death! How did you get back here so fast without my seeing you? And what are you doing on your knees cutting back the oregano instead of eating pumpkin pie with the rest of us?"

Jenny came into the house in something of a daze. How had she returned in time for dessert? How had so much happened in less than an hour? Was space time, or space non-time, continued under Krishnala's invisible dome even while it rested here on Earth? Was there such a time warp that Jenny could spend hours and hours there and return to Kansas proper with almost no time lapse?

Stop it, she ordered herself. You haven't even decided whether you made the whole thing up or not.

Lightly, she described the entire experience to Aunt Sally and Uncle John and Martha after the company had left.

"So what do you think?" Jenny asked. She of-

fered her own several interpretations of the whole business of Krishna-la.

"I have a favorite," said Uncle John. He lit his pipe calmly. Only the corner of his mouth twitched in an otherwise perfectly straight face. "My favorite theory is, and I do hope you won't find it too irritating, Jenny—my favorite theory is, that you've probably just lost your mind."

"That's a good theory," said Jenny. "It's even a logical interpretation, Uncle John."

"Or you could just be overtired, dear," said Aunt Sally. "Why not have a nap?"

Isn't it wonderful, Jenny thought, going upstairs to her bedroom to think things through. I have just had the most extraordinary experience of my life; and for an explanation, it appears I have a choice of something somewhere between overtired and out of my mind. Well, what did I expect? I hardly believed it myself entirely. Until just now, Jenny decided. Oddly enough, her relatives' disbelief made Jenny defend her own belief in Krishna-la.

Now all Jenny had to be sure of was whether the Krishna-lanians meant well, or—what? What was their purpose here on Earth? Why had they suddenly ejected her from the crystal city, when she asked the question about whether and how long they intended to hold her?

They obviously traveled a great deal about the universe, from galaxy to galaxy, even from galactic cluster to galactic cluster. They visited inhabited planets of all kinds, Allessi had indicated.

Compared to their ancient and sophisticated civilization, Earth was practically primitive. So was this just an inspection tour? Or did the Krishna-lanians have a mission? Most important, if they did have a mission, would it be harmful, even if only accidentally—because there didn't seem to be any malice in those Krishna-lanians she had met—to people on Earth?

And their labs—Jenny had a passion for labs—what did they look like? What were their information retrieval and storage systems?

Jenny's curiosity was growing overwhelming. The longer she sat in the middle of her patchwork quilt trying to think things through, the more questions she had.

Now she *was* getting overtired and crazy.

"Why are you plucking at the quilt like that?"

Martha struggled in through Jenny's bedroom door with a huge tray full of food. There were glasses of milk, pieces of pumpkin and apple pie, wedges of cheese, and two bars of chocolate.

Martha barely managed to stagger over to the bed with the laden tray, where she dumped the whole thing unceremoniously in front of her cousin.

"Don't ask me why my mother thinks people need a little something to eat right after Thanksgiving dinner to get their strength up," said Martha. "I only quote and deliver."

"To say nothing of Allessa's supper in Krishnala," Jenny said.

"Right," said Martha. "Say nothing."

"You don't believe?"

Martha considered Jenny's question, then made her own point.

"I've known you all my life. We were practically born on the same day. I feel this gives me a right to have an opinion. My opinion is, you are neither crazy nor overtired yet."

"Thank you," said Jenny, stuffed to the brim and biting into a piece of cheese anyway.

"I also think that if you don't get your questions answered, you will go crazy. And that will greatly overtire the rest of us," said Martha. "So my question is, when are you going back to Krishna-la?"

"In the morning," said Jenny. She paused midbite. "Want to come?"

"How would you feel," said Martha dryly, "if I said, another time?"

"I understand," said Jenny, laughing at Martha's quick exit from the room.

Martha loved to dream. She generally preferred to do this from a sitting, stationary position. Racing around a lot had never been Martha's idea of fun. But Jenny knew it wasn't fear, and it wasn't that she couldn't count on Martha if needed.

Fifteen minutes later, Jenny had showered and changed into her long, white nightgown. She and her mother drifted around the house at home in their long white nightgowns all winter, which made her father feel, he often said, as if he had taken up residence in a *Dracula* movie.

Jenny smiled at the memory of her parents and lay down.

Within seconds, she had the sensation she wasn't so much going to sleep as blacking out. Just before she went under, Jenny wondered in which world she would be when she finally woke.

CHAPTER 5

The Talking Cat

The silvery music of bells, the crystalline bed and walls curtained and canopied with endless yards of silky, white gauze billowing around her, and a purring pussycat with long fur the color of moonlight lying beside her—all were instant proof Jenny had been transported during the night.

She may have gone to bed Thanksgiving night in a farmhouse in Kansas. She had awakened the next day in a room at the Palace of the Winds in Krishnala. For the moment, she didn't care about any forebodings or any questions or any purposeful inquiry. She was filled with a quite exquisite and unaccountable feeling of happiness.

She was out of bed in a flash, peering behind the beautiful gauzy curtains through the crystal lace screens that were the windows of the space city's buildings.

The creature with the moonlight fur followed Jenny and then, with a gentle leap, landed on Jenny's shoulder.

"I ought to feel frightened, or at least cautious, you know," Jenny said to the cat. "It's funny, cat. All I feel is glad."

The purring cat purred louder and snuggled closer to her head.

"But where is everybody?" said Jenny. "I don't see a soul in the streets. And even if the walls are transparent crystal, I don't see anyone in any of the buildings down below in the city. I can't see a soul through my own bedroom walls here in this palace, for that matter. Where is everybody? Are they using their image deflectors so they appear not to be here? Why? What's so threatening about me? And why was I brought here if no one wants to be with me?"

"I want to be with you," said a voice quite close to Jenny's right ear.

"Cats do not speak English," said Jenny firmly. She didn't mind going a little crazy in a strange place. But she was definitely not going to go altogether up a tree.

"Probably not. But I do. I speak English."

The weight of the cat removed itself from Jenny's shoulder. It became Damon Lanza, standing beside

GEORGE WASHINGTON SCHOOL

her, solid and real and obviously delighted with himself.

"Damon Lanza," said Jenny, poking at him with an outraged finger, "if I'm to visit the Valley of the Blue Stars, I will not again expect to find you in my bedroom, especially while I'm still in my night-gown!"

"Nightgown? It's very pretty, whatever a night-gown is," said Damon Lanza, unperturbed.

Jenny realized manners here might be different from Earth manners, that Damon Lanza might see nothing wrong with wandering into a room where someone was sleeping. As for her nightgown, Jenny realized that actually here she was now dressed al-most like everybody else, in a pretty length of white, flowing cloth.

There was still, however, the business of the cat.

"Never mind about my nightgown, Damon Lanza. But my nerves aren't accustomed to your powers of cellular metamorphosis and your ability to change form at will. Please promise, when you're with me, not to be a cat or a bird or anything else but yourself."

"Fair enough," said Damon Lanza generously.

"Why can't I see anybody on the streets or in the houses?" said Jenny.

"People can create a non-see-through effect inside our buildings," said Damon Lanza, "by pushing a switch. It's as easy as pushing a switch on Earth to turn on an electric light. Our switches just make the walls like one-way mirrors."

"Marvelous," said Jenny. "And what about people on the streets?"

"Well, for one thing it's only six o'clock in the morning," said Damon Lanza, "early to be up. For another thing, we have underground cable cars in Krishna-la. So the few people who are up and about are whizzing about underground from place to place."

"One more question?" said Jenny. "I must sound such a pest."

"That's why I'm here," said Damon Lanza. "Allessi said I was to keep you company today. I'll show you our city and answer all your questions."

Damon Lanza's delight at this was so obvious, Jenny decided she needn't make any more apologies for herself. Besides, they'd brought her here, even in her sleep. They must want her.

"Well, then, my one question before breakfast," said Jenny. She was growing hungrier every minute in this wonderful, temperature-controlled air in which there wasn't a trace of Kansas winter, only perfect sunlight and gentle breezes. "My question is, how do you understand what I say, my English?"

"We all wear translators," said Damon Lanza.

From under his white tunic, he pulled out a small, button-like transreceiver on a chain. The tiny black and silver apparatus, Damon Lanza explained, translated instantly all languages everywhere into the sounds of Krishna-la. It also translated a Krishna-lanian's response back into the appropriate language.

"But it's all so fast," said Jenny. "And how does the conversation get to your brain from that button? To say nothing of in and out of your mouth!"

Damon Lanza laughed. "Don't forget, we aren't really put together the way we look to you," he said. "I don't think I could explain in English the way our real brains and bodies coordinate, together with our translators and image deflectors. Our minds are also connected to our community computer for quick information. There are other assorted communications systems between one another and our computer library."

"Maybe you could try to explain more?" said Jenny, taking Damon Lanza's arm. "But *after* breakfast. I don't know why, but I'm really starved this morning."

It was no hardship, keeping company with Damon Lanza. He—or at least the physical form he chose to inhabit—was tall, bronzed of skin, dark-eyed, with shiny black hair that fell to his shoulders. "Good thing I'm in love with Mike Ward," Jenny reminded herself several times that day.

Damon Lanza was a good and thorough host as well. After breakfast, he showed her not only the beautiful buildings and curious little shops of the city, but some things that interested Jenny even more. Krishna-la may have looked like a crystal ornament from a fairy-tale Christmas tree, but its science buildings were equipped with advanced technological systems. Jenny knew perfectly well that they were far beyond anything in the laboratories on Earth.

There was the main computer library. It had recording equipment Jenny had never seen before. The library, Damon Lanza explained, contained sociological, historical, biological, and cultural information about millions of inhabited planets throughout thousands of galaxies in the universe.

"We're aware of the fact that there is an unknown universe—or universes—but we haven't found a way to them yet," said Damon Lanza, almost apologetically.

"Right," said Jenny dryly, solemn-eyed.

There were long, crystal-roofed farms, miniature ecosystems that were combinations of hothouses for growing all necessary vegetables, medicinal herbs, and flowers for beauty. There were also fish tanks, not only for the purposes of having watery creatures to eat and enjoy, but for the condensation necessary to provide water for the long rows of plants.

Attached to the farms were biology labs for analyzing all kinds of tissues, and chemistry and physics labs for all kinds of research. There were cosmology and astronomy centers and specialized centers for medicine and surgery. There was the power plant, with a computer terminal that directed energy where needed in homes and laboratories and to the spaceships that required tremendous energy for travel.

"Can your translator handle the Krishna-lanian for mind-boggling?" said Jenny.

"That's a funny word," said Damon Lanza.

'It's a funny feeling," said Jenny.

They came out again into the sunlight that sparkled against the rock crystals of the city. Jenny's new dark glasses protected her eyes now, so she could enjoy the diamond brilliance.

They had taken up most of the morning seeing

what there was to see under the giant bubble of Krishna-la.

"We have an appointment for you now," said Damon Lanza lightly.

"An appointment?"

"The terminals at the computer library have been reserved for you for this afternoon," Damon Lanza explained.

The day was bright and sunny. The smile on Damon Lanza's face was happy and cheerful. Why was it that a slight chill went through Jenny Dean's heart?

CHAPTER 6

Computer Time

On the way to the computer library, Jenny had a chance to see the Krishna-lanian people going normally about their daily lives. They were all as beautiful as the Head of State family. Most were slender, with bronzed skin, dark hair and eyes, and physically fit. And since most were dressed in white tunics and trousers or caftans, Jenny continued to feel perfectly at home in her nightie.

Under one of the vast spired domes of the space city was the huge and airy computer library recording room with shelves of small, boxed tapes floor to ceiling. The room's single, central chair looked lonely in the middle of the recording equipment.

"No reason for making you black out this time, is there?" asked Allessa.

"Shall I answer aloud?" Jenny asked. "Truly, I don't mean to sound rude, Allessa. Since you can mentally read what I'm thinking, if I say what I'm thinking out loud, I'm repeating myself.''

Allessa's tinkling laughter was like music. "Oh, Jenny, it takes so much energy to telepath, translate, and all that. It would be so much easier if we could simply speak. We only read your mind the first time to get to know you better.''

"Good," said Jenny. She felt relieved. They may have felt no need for privacy in Krishna-la, but Jenny was still used to being able to close mental doors when she felt like it.

"In that case, no. I'd really rather not have a blackout if you don't mind," said Jenny. "Why did I need them before?''

"Only so you wouldn't be frightened by our ways of transportation, our recording equipment—all the things about Krishna-la that had to seem so strange to you at first," said Allessa.

"Well," said Jenny. "It's all still strange. But I don't think I'm as frightened. How did I get here so fast, by the way?''

"By transformer," said Allessa, as if, thought Jenny, she were saying 'by bus.' "We simply located you and transformed your matter into energy. Then we magnetized your energy here, and, so to speak, reassembled you.''

"Right," said Jenny, getting that glazed feeling

behind her eyes. It was a feeling she got whenever one of them explained a bit of advanced technology to her. There were moments she felt as a caveperson might have felt confronted with, say, a Mack truck.

As Allessa and Damon Lanza attached tiny, delicate electrodes to her temples, forehead, the base of her skull, wrists, heart, and the soles of her feet, Jenny's pulse began to race.

"Don't be afraid, Jenny," said Damon Lanza kindly. "It didn't hurt you yesterday. It won't hurt you today. It never hurts anyone."

"Why do I have the feeling something's going to be taken from me?" said Jenny. She felt little alarms going off inside her.

Allessi, tall and comforting, strode into the computer library in time to hear Jenny's last question.

"Only human," he teased Jenny gently. "You're all so grabby on planet Earth. You're all so afraid there isn't enough to go around. You don't share with each other."

"And then there really isn't enough to go around," said Jenny, seeing the point.

"Right," said Allessi.

He started the soft whirring sound that meant the recording machinery was in motion. All three stood comfortably close to Jenny in her chair.

"Sharing your information, all that wondrous information stored in your brain about Earth and its people and history and planets and animals—and yourself, of course—isn't going to deprive you of any of it," said Allessi. "We're only making a copy, not stealing the original."

Jenny felt reassured on that point. But she was still ill at ease about—what? The use Krishna-la would make of their collections of information? They had so many more powers than Earth people and they knew so many things Jenny couldn't even imagine. It probably meant she couldn't begin to imagine Krishna-la's purpose, either. But it didn't mean she wasn't going to try. Would a direct question help?

"What do you do with all of this information?" said Jenny as casually as possible.

"Learn," said Allessi promptly.

That's the whole thing? Jenny wondered silently. But Allessi said no more.

"Isn't *this* interesting," said Allessa. She was reading a bit of Jenny's taping.

Both she and Allessi had been making comments here and there on the readings from Jenny's brain as they were being recorded on tape.

"They have made so much technological progress on Earth in the last ten thousand years—indoor plumbing, rockets to the moon—and almost no progress at all in humanity. They still have wars; they still have hungry children,'' said Allessa.

Allessi nodded. ''Psychologically they are so primitive. It's hard to understand a species so dangerous to itself and so unhappy.''

''Why is that, Father, do you think?'' said Damon Lanza.

Jenny was beginning to feel like a bug under a microscope. ''It's my brain,'' she said. ''I'll answer that.''

The three listened attentively.

''I think it's because we're all so self-centered, so me-first,'' said Jenny. ''It's partly because we've inherited violence from the animal heritage. And it's partly because for thousands of years people on Earth have been saying that war is natural. So we've been taught to accept all that. Not people like Miss Casey, though—my English teacher. Or Captain Fisher. Or my parents. They know we can change.''

''So,'' said Allessi. ''Finally there is the beginning of some intelligence on Earth—not just intellect. An improvement over our last visit a couple of thousand years ago.''

Jenny felt pleased. She knew all too well the flaws

of her species. But she wanted the Krishna-lanians to see that at least some of her people were working at it.

It was a long session. It seemed to Jenny that the recordings from her brain filled one tape after another. She had no way of knowing how much time had passed. She had no way of knowing how much Earth time had passed.

Were people looking for her? This was a fascinating experience for her, but she knew it wasn't exactly fascinating to worry and wait at the other end of other people's fascinating experiences. She was growing tired, too. How much could they expect to get from one brain? A lot, Jenny knew. Many scientists believed each brain contained not only personal memory, but the memory of the whole human race back to its beginnings.

She was also aware that, scratch a few superficial differences, all human beings were pretty much like all others in their feelings of pain and joy. So for Allessi and Allessa, Jenny was a good example of everybody. So she gave information, and gave it, and gave it. Maybe something in Krishna-la's passion for learning would be of help in the universe.

But she was growing so tired. Couldn't they see how tired? And she was growing lonely, suddenly, too. She wanted—she wanted—to see another—human being. Lovely, here, in Krishna-la. Even wired to a machine, it was peaceful and lovely here. And yet—Jenny wanted the Earth, wanted her own kind. Would they let her go again? Or, this time, wouldn't they let her go again? So tired—

Then, for just a moment, Jenny saw an image. It was only a fleeting vision. She could not know if it was real or imagined. But just for a moment, she thought she saw Mike. He seemed quite near. He was smiling at her, holding out his hand.

And then it was over. She knew nothing more.

CHAPTER 7

Earth Visitor

When Jenny woke up, she had no idea how much time had passed. There just wasn't any way she could measure Earth time here in Krishna-la. It was like living in a time warp, a curve in which time looped back on itself.

She saw she was in the beautiful white gauzy bedroom she had awakened in that morning. She looked for the silvery white cat, for Damon Lanza. There was nothing, no one—just utter silence. Jenny slept again.

"Hey, sleepy head. How long are you going to just lie there?"

The loved and familiar voice startled Jenny awake. She opened her eyes to darkening skies— was it Friday night now?—and the lamplit coziness of her palace bedroom, and, best of all, Mike Ward.

There he was, standing at the foot of her bed, his

dark, curling hair, golden eyes, and tall, muscular body filling Jenny with the most wonderful mixture of joy and security.

"Mike!" she cried, jumping up from the pillows and galloping down the bed toward him. "What are you doing here? How did you get here? Am I glad to see you!"

"I wouldn't have guessed," said Mike dryly and very fondly as the small girl with the mop of blond hair leaped from the bed into his arms.

"He got here because we found him in your head," said Allessi.

The Head of State strolled into Jenny's room with Allessa right behind him.

"Your brain told us you were lonely, Jenny," said Allessa. "This seemed to be the person you mentioned most in your memory tapes."

"He also happened to be nearby, so it was very easy to pluck him in, as it were," said Allessi.

"I came to the farm to pay you a surprise visit," said Mike. "What I found was no Jenny, and an invisible force field protecting an area ten miles north and south, and five miles east and west. You can *bet* I'd be nearby, looking for you."

"His mind was open, like yours was, so it was easy to bring him in," said Allessi. "He had also begun to make some connections."

"Connections?" Jenny asked.

"Television news people have been talking all day about an out-of-season cyclone in this area," said Mike. "They've also been talking about a new object spotted near Alpha Centauri. Scientists can't decide whether it's an asteroid, a moon they missed, or just a bit of cosmic debris—or maybe a visitor from another part of the universe, according to the more imaginative cosmologists."

Allessi enjoyed that a lot. "It's our image deflectors at work. We've deflected the image of Krishnala four and a half light-years away to Alpha Centauri so no one will suspect we're here," he explained to Mike. "As for the out-of-season cyclone—it was an excellent Earth phenomenon we used to hide our settling-in dust, so to speak."

"Whatever the actual explanations," said Mike, "I couldn't help connecting Jenny's disappearance with the force field and the news reports. Jenny has always had a magnetic pull toward unusual happenings."

"She is an unusual girl," said Allessa, "so bright, so eager to be of service."

"So interested in everything," said Allessi.

"True," said Jenny, "and one thing that interests me is how come I blacked out again?"

"You didn't black out," said Allessa quickly.

"After all that recording, your brain was so over-tired, it just went to sleep."

Was Allessa's answer too quick, wondered Jenny. Or am I just a bit overtired as she says? At any rate, Jenny decided, it was just wonderful having Mike here. She felt less wary already.

Mike, however, was wary enough for both of them, though Jenny didn't find that out until later that evening.

"What did you mean before, when you said that Mike's mind was open, like mine was?" Jenny asked Allessi.

"We can't bring in anyone who doesn't want to come," Allessi answered. "As we probe someone's mind, we discover whether there's a willingness to come to Krishna-la or not. Without a kind of invitation, so to speak, we cannot enter someone's heart or transport someone through our protective shield."

"Mind probe?" said Mike. "What do you mean, mind probe?"

Jenny laughed.

"It's amazing here," she said. "Any question gets answered. Any answer begs more questions."

Allessa laughed too. "We're telepaths, Mike, that's all. Nothing any brain can't get the knack of."

That evening after dinner at the large, round plexiglass table in the main palace hall, Damon Lanza, Mara, and Dora showed Mike everything Damon Lanza had shown Jenny earlier that morning. Though it was dark outside the bubble protecting Krishna-la, the space city's incredible energy plant carried enough power to floodlight any building Mike wanted to see.

Mike was, of course, as fascinated as Jenny was, but along with his obvious fascination, she could see Mike's smile grow more and more fixed. As they walked between the crystal-roofed farms and the power plant's computer terminal, Jenny had a chance to whisper, "What's the matter? I know that smile. You get it every time you have to swallow something you absolutely hate, like my father's squash."

"Right," said Mike.

"Are you going to explain?" said Jenny.

Mara and Dora skipped along to Mike's side, each one taking an arm and preventing any further private conversation for a while.

After that, Damon Lanza occupied Jenny's attention as they all went to the vast domed theater of Krishna-la.

"We don't want you to think all that occupies us

is space travel and documentation,'' said Damon Lanza.

The five stayed to see the late show, a televised broadcast of a sort of outer-space western on a screen Jenny judged to be fifty feet high.

''Nice to see that even here, the guys from the good planets outdo the guys from the bad planets,'' said Jenny. ''Also nice to see trickery and mental footwork, instead of weapons.''

''There are all different kinds of weapons, Jen,'' said Mike oddly.

On the way back to the palace, they managed another moment alone together.

''What's the matter, Mike?'' Jenny insisted.

''This place worries me,'' said Mike. ''It's nice, they're nice, Allessi and Allessa are nice—everything's nice. But all this niceness makes me nervous. I mean, we can't even get out of here without their letting us go. And however nice a prison is, Jen, a prison is a prison is a prison.''

''But I've been let go,'' said Jenny. ''I was let back to the farm.''

''Here you are again, though, aren't you?'' said Mike. ''And so am I.''

They entered the palace hall then and saw what it held with a shock. ''And look who else they've got,'' said Mike. ''This is creepy! Look who else.''

CHAPTER 8

Friendly Arrivals

There, in the main hall of the Palace of the Winds, were three out of the other five people in the world Jenny was closest to.

Before entering, Jenny turned with a questioning glance to Allessi.

"Got them right out of your head, m'dear," said the Head of State. "Now you won't be lonely at all. Only your parents seemed unwilling to leave their practices. Your mother has two new patients, one a schizophrenic child, I believe. Your father didn't want to leave a heifer suspected of having anthrax."

"But your best friend, Laurie Harper, was willing to come, and Mike's best friend, Joe Scott, was willing," said Allessa. "And since we taped a great deal about a Captain Ray Fisher, we brought him as well."

"How?" said Mike. His eyebrows knit in a single, severe line. Mike, who had a passion for

71

freedom, Jenny knew, reacted badly when he suspected people of meddling with other people's lives.

"Just a simple, long-distance thought implant—
the way you on Earth would use a telephone—
suggesting they might like to visit us," said Allessi.

They entered the main hall then and surprised
their newly arrived guests.

"Jenny!" Laurie's dramatic voice called out at
the sight of her friend. "Jenny, I don't care nearly as
much what we're all doing in this *bizarre* place as I
do that you're *standing* there in your *nightgown*!"

Laurie Harper, in tailored jeans and a perfectly
cut jacket, came bounding over to hug Jenny. Laurie
was tall, thin, beautiful, elegant, and sensible. She
was also an athlete, captain of the basketball team,
and an A student—everything, in short, Jenny always said, you'd want in a friend, including the
patience to be friends with me. True, Laurie would
agree.

"Never mind Jenny in a nightgown. What are you
doing in one?" said Joe Scott, coming forward to
clap a hand on Mike's shoulder.

"This is not a nightgown, it's a toga," Mike said
stiffly. "You'll find togas a lot more comfortable
than what we wear." Mike had been given a toga on
arrival.

Joe Scott was handsome, black, popular president

of the Student Council, and liked being all three. He also was almost a professional actor and, like Laurie Harper, enjoyed nice clothes.

"Actually," said Joe. "Actually, the toga's wonderfully cut, and I do have the shoulders for it."

"Do you think," Mike said, turning to Jenny, "the healthy air of Krishna-la will have any ego-deflating effect on this personal friend of ours?"

Captain Ray Fisher, who waited serenely for people and things to come to him, stood in his usual black turtleneck and tweeds, chatting with Mara and Dora. Jenny ran over to the tall, kind man, whose warm eyes and lean, bony face she adored. The detective was a study in contrasts. He was gentle of manner—Jenny saw him as a guardian angel of truth and compassion who kept Winter Falls in reasonably nonviolent condition by thinking things out logically rather than shooting them out. The captain never ever carried a gun. But he could look like the devil when he was angry at Law and Order politicians, for instance, or at cruelty of any kind.

"Jenny, this is going to be fascinating," said the captain. "With my interest in magic and science, this whole experience looks as if it's going to be a wonderful combination of both. Thank you for thinking me here."

"It will," said Allessi, opening his arms wide in a

gesturing welcome to his five visitors, "be a wonderful combination of magic and science for you all. How well put, Captain Fisher."

Allessa came forward then, to second her husband's greeting. "We will do everything we can to entertain you all. We hope you will allow us to study you as we have Jenny, to learn about Earth and its people through your minds. In return, we will teach you what we know, what we can—and, I hope, amuse you well."

"Amuse us well, or charm us with spells so we won't or can't leave," grumbled Mike.

"Well," Jenny said to Mike in a low voice, "we are five of us now, at least. Whatever happens, no one of us has to face it alone."

"It's late," said Allessa. "May I show each of you to your bedroom? Before we show our newest visitors whatever they wish to see in Krishna-la, a good night's rest might be welcome."

"See?" said Mike. "We're being separated already."

Mike was right. Their rooms were far apart along the long crystal halls of the palace. "I remember where your room is, Jen. I'll be there in a minute if you need me."

Jenny watched as Allessi escorted the captain far,

far down the corridor. She watched where Allessa showed Laurie her room around the corner and along a different hall. She saw Damon Lanza take Mike and Joe off in still another direction from either her own room or any of the others. And she wondered if Mike had made his point well.

"Silly, it's just silly to think we're being separated on purpose," said Jenny to the high, white gauzy curtains, to her beautifully white-draperied bed, to the soft, dark eternal spring of the Krishna-la night. She looked out through the crystal lace-work window at the moonlight, at the beauty of the shining buildings. It was all so lovely and so peaceful.

Mike's worries were just shadows with no substance. The purpose of Krishna-la wasn't to scare or control them.

But if that were true, why, several hours later, had one of them completely disappeared?

CHAPTER 9

Laurie Is Missing

It was Laurie. When Jenny woke the next morning, Laurie was gone.

Anxious to see her friend, Jenny had run down the palace hallway. But Laurie's high, crystal-walled room with the gauzy hangings, just like Jenny's own, was empty. Downstairs, the big hall where the people of the Palace of the Winds dined, was empty, too.

"Am I earlier than everybody? Or later?" Jenny said aloud.

She could see the sun through the clear bubble that protected Krishna-la for miles. Its position in Earth's sky told Jenny it wasn't much past seven o'clock in the morning. Saturday, wasn't it? Jenny felt already she'd been in Krishna-la a very long time.

But where could Laurie be so early? Had she gone

somewhere on her own? Or had she been taken away? And where was everyone else?

"Good morning, Jenny."

A voice came out of the middle of the empty room.

"Who's there?" Jenny asked quickly, looking around.

"Ah, I'm so sorry," said the voice. "I must have forgotten to turn off my image deflector again."

It was Allessa, suddenly and cheerfully appearing at the table with ten plates and napkins.

"Here I am," said Allessa.

"Yes," said Jenny. "Here you are. But Laurie, where's Laurie?"

"I'm sure wherever she is, she's just fine," said Allessa, still and as always cheerful.

Too cheerful? Jenny wondered. Then she wondered why she kept on wondering about such a peaceful, beautiful place as Krishna-la. It was so full of peaceful, beautiful people and so much more advanced and civilized than Earth.

But wonder Jenny did, each time anything out of the way happened. Laurie going off without a word, for instance, was out of the way. Should she go upstairs for Mike and Joe? Or the captain? No. No need to disturb them so early, or to worry them yet.

Mike was already suspicious of this lovely miracle of a city.

As for Jenny, she just wasn't sure. Krishna-la was either a messenger from other intelligent life in space, a promise of the possibility of future peace. Or, Krishna-la had a purpose here Jenny, and everyone else on Earth, had better learn about before—before what? Before they all got tricked into some sort of surrender to the Krishna-lanians!

"Not hungry?" Allessa called after Jenny.

But Jenny was already out into the sunlit courtyard of the Palace of the Winds, and off to search the crystal city from beyond the stars for her missing friend.

There was an archway in the plaza below the palace Jenny hadn't seen before. On an impulse, like a curious Alice in a Starship Wonderland, Jenny darted through the arch.

She found herself, half running, half stumbling, down a steep tunnel remarkably like the long airlock chambers she had seen in pictures of interplanetary spaceships. The walls of the tunnel were lined with what looked like one-person space pods. The pods had complicated read-out panels and instruments, but no arms Jenny could see. Were the pods for leaving the spaceship city to explore this or that planetary surface? To collect sample specimens of rocks and plants? To collect what else? People, for instance?

What else was down here? Jenny's curiosity and talent for observation had never been more alert. As she wandered on in the strange lavender light of the tunnel, Jenny realized that Krishna-la wasn't protected only by the dome of the half bubble visible aboveground. The city, she could now see, was encased in a wholly round bubble, half of it underground. The underground half was full of equipment too complicated for Jenny to understand. She could only register and describe the stuff later, she decided.

She had a hunch she shouldn't be down here at all, for some reason. For whatever reason, she proved a few seconds later that she was right. Behind her, she heard running feet. The feet belonged to four guards, who promptly and quietly surrounded her. Instantly, something soft covered her face.

There was no way of knowing how long she'd been out. When Jenny came to, she was right back up on the city's surface again. The guards had disappeared, and she was groggy with whatever they had used to knock her out.

If Krishna-la was innocent, Jenny was wondering

again, why the secrecy over whatever was below the city's surface?

And still—where was Laurie?

Two more streets and another flowered plaza, and then Jenny finally found her.

There was Laurie, happily, it seemed, and completely absorbed in a clothing boutique across the cobbled square.

"What are you doing here?" said Jenny, entering the small, pretty shop.

"Isn't it wonderful? Aren't these things too divine? Aren't you going to remove that nightgown instantly and try on everything? They're going to let me do the ordering. I can choose from all these clothes catalogs," said Laurie.

"You don't generally babble, from excitement or anything else," said Jenny.

"I'm babbling now," said Laurie. "I've dreamed of running a boutique my whole life. Imagine, endless supplies of clothes to choose from, to help other people look marvelous. Oh, Jenny, such fun, don't you think?"

Laurie was holding up a soft, rose tunic with a matching rose-flowered scarf to belt in the waist. "Heaven?" she asked.

"Ah, yes." The answer came from a Krishna-lanian woman who had just entered the shop. Like most Krishna-lanians, she was tall, dark-haired, and slender. "The rose color would suit me so well, don't you think?" she said.

Laurie and her customer seemed enchanted with the material, the tunic, and each other's passion for dresses, shoes, scarves, and the exact drape of the tunic's fabric.

Jenny interrupted Laurie's bliss to ask a question. "How did you get here?"

Laurie paused to consider while expertly winding a length of pale blue chiffon around the woman's hair. "I don't know, Jenny, to tell the truth," Laurie said. "I woke up. It was so lovely outside. I ran into the courtyard, and my steps brought me here. When I arrived, the lady in the boutique asked me whether I loved clothes as much as I seemed to, and if so, whether I'd run the shop for her."

Then Laurie smiled such a happy smile, Jenny could hardly begin to get analytical without destroying her friend's pleasure.

"Well," said Jenny. "Have fun. See you later."

She wasn't even certain Laurie heard her, because Laurie's attention was so quickly reabsorbed in the boutique and the three new customers who had just come in.

Jenny decided to go back to the palace and share all she'd seen that morning with Mike or Joe or Captain Fisher. She wanted some reaction besides her own.

Only, when she got back to the Palace of the Winds on the hill, all of them were gone.

CHAPTER 10

Living Out Fantasies

Now what had these alien intelligences done with her friends?

Were they attached to the terminals over at the computer library, while their minds were probed, their bodies mapped, their tastes and possibilities and interests analyzed? Or were they off, like Laurie, pursuing those interests?

"And if they are pursuing their own interests," Jenny muttered, circling the round, icy table in the great hall, "are they doing it of their own free will? Or are they obeying sets of silent orders sent to their brains by Allessi?" At any rate, thought Jenny, knowing them as I do, they shouldn't be hard to find.

Joe Scott was the easiest. All she had to do was go on over to the domed theater where they'd been the night before.

Jenny's guess was right. Joe, like Laurie, was pursuing his favorite interest, easily discoverable by any mind-reading inhabitant of Krishna-la, even without machinery.

"Jenny, come see," Joe called, as she opened the door at the rear of center aisle. "Look at this stage. Look at the lighting I've got to work with. Isn't it marvelous? They're allowing me to be guest producer, of whatever play I like. What a terrific company!"

"Terrific," said Jenny.

"I'm going to do *Hamlet*," said Joe.

"Terrific," said Jenny.

"But without any of the killings," said Joe.

"That's really terrific," said Jenny. "How do you do *Hamlet*, which, as I remember from English class, has six major deaths, without any killings?"

"Simple," said Joe. "They all use their image deflectors."

Joe was clearly so pleased with himself, Jenny didn't have the heart to discuss her friend's outer-space version of Shakespeare's play.

"Right," said Jenny. "Seen Mike?"

"Went off with the captain, I think," said Joe, returning to the company of actors who smiled with pleasure at their new producer.

"He's in heaven," Jenny mentioned in passing.

Then she stopped short as she left the theater. "Heaven," she repeated. "Is that where we are, in some kind of heaven, where wishes and other things come true?"

She felt the urgency, suddenly, to find Mike, and the captain most of all. The captain was the most intelligent human being Jenny knew. She needed that intelligence now.

But what was the captain's idea of heaven? What interest would he most like to pursue, and Allessi be most quick to grant him?

Science, magic, music, those were the captain's interests, and the logical working out of often illogical behavior. Mental strategy was Captain Fisher's favorite part of police detective work, Jenny had observed. What else had she observed?

As she was thinking, Jenny had wandered over to the complex of science buildings. No guards prevented her from entering here. As she wandered into the familiar computer library, she remembered something else. The few hours from time to time when the captain wasn't working on some new bio-psychological theory, practicing magic tricks, or playing his classical guitar, he could be found taking pleasure in the mental strategy of a chess game.

"Do Krishna-lanians play games?" Jenny asked someone going from one laboratory to another.

"Yes, sometimes," came the courteous reply.

"Would there be a special place? A room, or building?" said Jenny.

"About a mile into the hills from the plaza below the palace," said the young woman scientist, "there's the Recreation Dome. Under the dome there are indoor games, and in the fields below, we play outdoor games."

"Thank you," said Jenny.

It was the first walk Jenny had taken into the lush, green fields of Krishna-la. There were pastures of cows and slopes for the sheep, meadows of horses, and groves and gardens of trees and flowers everywhere.

As Jenny had guessed, Captain Fisher had found his game, and not only his game, but a heavenly combination of everything he loved best.

"Look at this, Jenny," said the captain, eyes warm with interest.

Under the crystalline Recreation Dome, the captain had found a crystalline chess game with pieces almost as large as a man. He had also found a music synthesizer, guitar, and all the wire equipment he needed to set up his musical chess game.

"Isn't this something? Listen to this," he said. "I can play chess, move the pieces to the chords of this guitar. Terrific?"

"Terrific," said Jenny for the fourth time that morning.

The captain had found a magical, scientific, musical chess game. His attention was captured. Jenny tried several times to interest him in a discussion of the pros and cons of the attitudes of Krishna-la. Nothing happened. The captain was completely absorbed in his chess game.

"So much for my need for an intelligent reaction," Jenny said to the air.

"Beg pardon?" said the captain.

"What I want to know is why we are being given whatever we like?" said Jenny, trying one last time.

"Absolutely," said the captain. "Look what this A7th chord does to the Queen's bishop."

"Absolutely," said Jenny. "Where's Mike?"

"Went off with—someone, I think," said Captain Fisher.

"Truly perceptive," said Jenny.

"Truly," said the captain.

"I'm not going mad," said Jenny. "Not me."

But she thought she'd better leave the Recreation Dome just in case. Laurie had been deeply absorbed

in her boutique. Joe had been completely absorbed in his theatrical production. Captain Fisher could hardly hear Jenny, he was so involved with his musical chess game.

Jenny found the same questions going through her head. Were they absorbed because they were happy, happy doing what they wanted to do? Or was there something in Krishna-la controlling their minds, and if so, what for?

She didn't expect any more attention from Mike than she'd gotten from the other three, but she had to try.

Jenny found him—naturally—on a small farm beyond the hills. He was completely absorbed in a discussion with two Krishna-lanian agriculturalists and a veterinarian on breech-birthing techniques.

"Hi," said Mike when he saw Jenny.

It was the only word he addressed to her for the twenty minutes she stood there, plucking at his sleeve, smiling and trying to get his attention.

"Short of clubbing him with a pole ax, I give up," she said, again into the Krishna-lanian air.

And then, it happened to her.

In the secret part of her mind, where people treasure what they love most, Jenny had dreamed always of rocky, snow-capped mountains where only the tiny mountain deer and goats and marmosets climbed and played on the high, green pastures and among the rocky crags.

Somehow, walking back among the hills, Jenny found herself in just such a place. There, she was caught by such joy, such lightness of spirit, such a sense of deep absorption that she never, never wanted to leave again.

She understood entirely now the happiness of the others. She, too, was completely and absolutely enchanted. Jenny's mind, like the others, was held by Krishna-la.

Somewhere, dimly she remembered that she had set out that morning to find out whether she and the others, maybe the rest of Earth, had to be alerted. She remembered wondering if what went on in Krishna-la were real or mere illusion, like the shapes of the bodies of Krishna-lanians. And were they illusions? Were all these wonderful dreams gifts— or snares to control?

Jenny pushed away those dim rememberings. She pushed until they were gone. Nothing mattered now except the magic of the mountains, and the joy she wanted to stay here and feel forever.

CHAPTER 11

Violence Strikes

There was no way for Jenny to know, in the time that followed, whether hours passed, or days, or even weeks.

Laurie had her clothes shop. Joe had his theater. Mike had his animals. Captain Ray Fisher had his magically scientific musical chess games.

As for Jenny, she had her mountains and her wild creatures. She was even filled with her favorite emotion, a kind of feverish joy she loved to feel, as others might love peace or excitement or laughter.

They all did as they wished all day, except for the two hours each afternoon—or so the schedule seemed to Jenny—when the five of them were hooked up to separate computer terminals. For those two hours, their minds and bodies were monitored and diagrammed. Their thoughts, feelings, and body responses were taped and stored in the computer library system of Krishna-la.

The tall, gracious Heads of State, Allessi and Allessa, were also excellent scientists. Jenny and her friends were not only entertained, they were studied by experts.

"Is it hours—or days—since I wondered whether we're all here because we want to be, or because we're being lulled into a false sense of security and we're actually prisoners?" said Jenny to Mike during an interval between tests.

"Who cares?" said Laurie, sighing from her chair across the lab at the thought of returning to her lovely shop.

"Right," said Mike, "who cares?" His golden eyes smiled at Jenny in contentment, while Joe Scott next to him nodded and agreed, "Who cares?"

Only the captain was left for Jenny to turn to for a response.

"How long has it been, Captain, since I've wondered if we'll ever be allowed to leave?" said Jenny, turning her head in her wired chair to the captain in his. "I mean, what do you think are the chances that instead of being allowed to go home one of these days, we'll all end up being swept out into space to a faraway galaxy? I mean, what happens to us when

Krishna-la itself leaves Earth and our own Milky Way galaxy forever?''

The captain, usually alert and serious, smiled at Jenny, completely relaxed.

"How about—back there, back home?'' Jenny said. "Your cases, for instance.''

"They'll keep,'' said the captain. "We're here now, and it's fascinating. We're witnessing the one thing anyone on Earth who looks beyond his own nose cares about—the answer to the question: Is there intelligence besides our own in this universe? It's fascinating to know the answer is yes, isn't it, Jenny?''

"But what if—''

This time nobody answered Jenny's probes. Nobody seemed to care.

A series of blissful sighs and smiles, even from the captain, were the only response to Jenny's worries. And then, even Jenny stopped worrying and wondering. Even Jenny stopped probing. They were in Paradise. It was enough.

It was enough until the afternoon the fighting started.

They were sitting under a large, spreading tree that sheltered them from the bright glare of the sun. It was just after one of their computer library sessions. They were all hungry, and they had decided to bring a picnic lunch to Krishna-la's pretty foothills before returning to their separate interests.

Jenny and Laurie had been chatting idly about how bizarre it felt, knowing their thoughts were all on tape for another civilization to read about.

The men, Jenny could overhear, were chatting, equally idly, she thought, about history on Earth, about its wars and violence.

She had overheard bits and pieces of the conversation as they ate lunch from the big hamper. The captain and Mike, in particular, had been discussing various horrors and atrocities.

"You know," said Jenny at one point, "your point of view may be that war never solved anything. But your descriptions are quite gruesome, especially considering we're eating lunch."

Mike laughed. But soon, they were discussing the horrors of war again. "The attitudes are even dumber than the ways," said Mike. "Imagine brother killing brother in the name of Brotherhood, anyone at all killing in the name of God, making war under the banner of bringing peace. Do you remember—"

And the discussion was off again, until Jenny and Laurie moved off a bit to eat their lunch in peace.

That peace lasted for only a little while. After lunch, Mike and Joe took off for a walk to stretch their legs. Only Mike returned.

He came running back to where Jenny and Laurie and the captain were still relaxing under the tree. He was running, not for pleasure, but as if he were being chased. He kept looking over his shoulder.

"What is it, Mike?" Jenny cried out. "Mike, you've got a cut lip. You're bleeding. What's happened? Where's Joe?"

"You're not going to believe this," said Mike. "Here we are in a city from a space civilization dedicated to nonviolence, and Joe and I have just been beaten up."

"By whom? Where?" said Captain Fisher. His handsome face was once again serious; his lean muscled body was ready for action.

Mike, bruised, but equally strong and fit, stood ready at the captain's side to go rescue his friend.

"Tell us where you're going so Laurie and I can follow," said Jenny. "What's going on, Mike?"

"Just over that hill, Joe and I were walking along, discussing some of the tribal wars in Africa, when the tallest Masai warrior you've ever seen in your life attacked Joe. Of course, I started to help Joe out. I tried to think about my judo class and the defense

holds and movements that would work best. But just then, out jumped two Japanese samurai from somewhere who immediately began attacking me.'' Mike rubbed his jaw. ''Thank goodness, Joe had helped me out in judo class. I managed to fight them off, even if they did get me a couple of times.''

''What happened to Joe, Mike?'' said Laurie, as they all headed out over the hill to rescue Joe.

''I don't know,'' said Mike. ''When I turned around to help him fend off the Masai warrior, both Joe and the warrior had disappeared.''

''Show us the place, Mike,'' said the captain. ''We'll find footsteps, something, don't worry.''

At that, Mike and Captain Fisher shot out ahead of the girls, over the hill and out of their sight.

''We'll keep after them,'' said Jenny. ''They may need us for something. Besides, I'm too worried to just wait here.''

''Right,'' said Laurie. ''Only for heavens' sake, Jen, tuck up that nightie before you break a leg.''

Jenny hugged her friend. Laurie wasn't frivolous. She made jokes to cover her most real concerns, her friends.

''Joe will be all right, Laurie,'' said Jenny. ''We'll find him.''

But as Jenny and Laurie sped on and crested the

hill, they soon realized that not only had Joe disappeared but Mike had, too.

The girls found out what happened from the captain, whom they discovered nearly unconscious and badly hurt. He was lying behind an outcropping of rocks on the other side of the hill.

''Who did this?'' said an angry Jenny, cradling the captain's head. ''Who did this to you?''

CHAPTER 12

The Battle Rages

"You're not going to believe this," said the captain. "I'm not sure I do. But I've just been knocked about by a small medieval army. I don't remember all of them. But I'm certain I saw a king and queen and knights and foot soldiers."

"What is a medieval army of five hundred years ago doing in the middle of a space city of the future?" Laurie wondered.

"Now it's my turn not to care about explanations," said Jenny, still angry. "How dare they punch out the captain!" She was ready now to punch back. Never mind all their long discussions on finding other ways than violence to meet violence.

Bruised as the captain's face was, he had a quick laugh for his favorite young friend.

"Come on," he said, getting painfully to his feet. "Let's go after Mike and Joe."

"You go on with Laurie, Captain," said Jenny.

"Are you sure nothing's broken?"

"Nothing's broken," said the captain "Where are you going?"

"Back for help," said Jenny. "I'm going to get Damon Lanza and Mara and Dora and whoever else will come. I want to ask Allessi some questions, too, if I can find him, about what's with Masai and samurai and knights and foot soldiers among the peaceful hills of Krishna-la."

"Good thinking," said the captain. "Be careful, Jenny. You'll be alone till you get back to town. And these hills are full of surprises all of a sudden."

"Right," said Jenny. "You two be careful, too."

Jenny watched Captain Fisher and Laurie disappear over the huge rocky boulders off to the left.

As she turned to the right she saw a much larger army than the captain had described coming from the Krishna-la forest and heading toward the hills. And these weren't medieval foot soldiers or knights on horses, either. This was a modern, fully armed and outfitted battalion of khaki-uniformed infantry. These soldiers didn't look as if they were out on weekend maneuvers. They looked, decided Jenny, with a shiver crawling up her spine, thoroughly ready for real and armed combat. What was going on here?

As half a dozen tanks poured out of the forest

after the rifle-carrying infantry, Jenny turned and sprinted for the city.

"I haven't been this angry in I don't know when," Jenny said when she found Damon Lanza.

"Look at those fists," said Damon Lanza. He pointed to Jenny's clenched hands. "I thought, like us, you were beyond violence."

"I don't know about actual violence," said Jenny. "But I'm certainly not beyond getting angry. What's going on in Krishna-la? Why are my friends being roughed up? What's that army doing out there coming across the fields from the forest? Who are they after?"

"Us, I suspect," said Damon Lanza simply.

"Oh dear, oh, I never thought of that," said Jenny. Instantly, she was no longer angry at Damon Lanza and the Krishna-lanians. Instantly, she was apologetic. "I never thought, truly I didn't—oh, I'm so sorry, I never realized Earth people would come, or that if they did, they'd attack."

"Yes, well—" Damon Lanza began.

"Of course, you don't know what to say," said Jenny. "I wouldn't either, I'd be so upset. Well, we've got to try to fend them off. We can't let them near this beautiful city, Damon Lanza. Come on, let's find Allessi and Allessa. They'll know what to do. Has this happened before? What do Krishna-lanians do when they're attacked? Oh, how do I apologize for Earth people? They're—we're such barbarians, always trying to destroy what we don't understand."

Jenny was running as she spoke, distraught with sorrow for this Earth attack on Krishna-la.

"We'll help defend you, of course," said Jenny to Allessi when she found him at lunch at the round crystal table in the palace hall. "I know I speak for us all, the captain and Mike and Joe and Laurie. And you know you can depend on me."

"Jenny, my dear," said the tall, gentle Head of State, wiping his mouth. "As you know, we don't fight here."

"Yes, I understand that," said Jenny. "But you do defend yourselves, don't you? Krishna-la has survived so many thousands, hundreds of thousands of years, you must have been through this before. What do you do? Whatever you do, we'll help."

"Thank you, Jenny. Damon Lanza, get Dora and Mara. The three of you can give Jenny and her friends lessons in using our image deflectors," said Allessi, rising from his luncheon. "And lessons also in cellular metamorphosis in case they want to change shape."

Jenny thought it odd Allessi seemed so little troubled by her report of the large army. And she had forgotten to mention the Masai warrior or the samurai judo masters on the warpath. Where had they come from? But this was no time to discuss the finer points, while a graver attack was under way.

"On your way now, you two," said Allessi. "I'll go alert our own forces to cope with things in our own way."

Damon Lanza and Jenny found Mara and Dora in the larger of the greenhouses picking cucumbers for dinner salads. When they were told the news, they seemed a lot more concerned than their father.

Each checked out the small, transistorized control box at her waist. Jenny saw each temporarily disappear from view, then appear again where she'd been.

"We're okay," said Mara, who'd been picking up Earth slang in the past few days. "Let's get image deflectors for the rest."

Damon Lanza collected five of the small boxes with their waist clips from the storeroom at the Palace of the Winds. If Jenny hadn't been so worried about Mike and Joe, she'd have enjoyed her lessons in making not herself but her image disappear from one place and appear in another.

She learned now as the four of them left the city for the hills. Cellular metamorphosis was impossible. And image deflection took practice. It took practice, Jenny discovered, to deflect her image precisely where she wanted it.

"Project your image in front of a rock, for instance," said Damon Lanza, "and anyone coming toward your image fast will hurt himself on the rock as he attacks thin air where he thinks you are. Gives you time to get even farther away. Also, it takes practice to keep your image projected. It has a tendency to merge back with your actual physical self."

By the time they got outside the city, the young people discovered pandemonium in the fields between the forest and the hills. The noise of thousands of soldiers was deafening. The shots being fired, the maneuvering of the tanks roaring around, the yelling from the attacking army were horrendous. Smoke was here and there, and a few fires had broken out. Jenny noticed no obvious plan of action or attack. The army seemed to be racing in circles.

The trouble, obviously, was that the few hundred Krishna-lanians, marshaled from their jobs and still wearing their lovely white tunics, ought to have been easy targets—and they weren't! They were on

one side of the field, then the other, never still long enough for the Earth army to take good aim. Only a few hundred Krishna-lanians were up against a couple of thousand soldiers, but the Krishna-lanians' speed was incredible. They continually moved out of range, while managing to divert the army's attention from the city. The people of the shining crystal city didn't want the slightest crack or splinter in a single crystal wall.

If the guns, smoke, and fire hadn't been so real, Jenny might have found the scene kind of funny.

"Look at that," she said to Mara. "How backward killers are compared to people who think problems through rather than shoot them out. Look at how frustrated the soldiers are, trying to find a target and hitting nothing but empty air."

Mara laughed, and so did Dora.

Then, nothing anymore was funny. Across the field, Jenny saw Mike go down. In the heat of battle, Jenny had watched Damon Lanza instruct Laurie, the captain, and even Joe, how to use the deflectors. But Damon Lanza hadn't had enough time to get to Mike Ward.

Now it was too late. Jenny screamed as the one person dearest to her in the world was shot and killed.

CHAPTER 13

Insight

In a flash, Jenny was across the field and kneeling down by Mike's side. The bullet had entered his chest and pierced his heart. A rage more terrible than before, more terrible than anything she had ever felt, gripped Jenny. In tears, she flung her image deflector away and swept up a fallen rifle and an abandoned machine gun. She wanted to destroy whoever had destroyed what she loved most.

"Don't."

The captain, still limping, laid a hand gently but firmly on her arm. In the lean face, the warm eyes looked deeply into Jenny's own.

"Don't, Jenny," said the captain. "You won't be able to live with it if you should happen to kill."

From the hills, a herd of tiny, chamois goats scampered in fear away from the thundering sounds of war. There was a sharp, brutal blast. The tiny creatures dropped in an instant.

"Did you see that, Captain?" Jenny was trembling with grief and rage now. "I can't live with that sight, either."

The captain tightened his clasp in affection and understanding, and left Jenny's side to pick up Mike and carry him off the field.

Damon Lanza and Laurie were together over near the forest, sabotaging the enemy soldiers as they came through the trees. With their image deflectors, Damon Lanza and Laurie kept distracting squads of infantry, making them dart in the wrong direction.

Joe Scott, looking badly hurt, judging by his crookedly held arm, was with a large group of young, Krishna-lanian defenders at the foot of the hills. They were engaged in diverting troops from the town's outlying buildings.

Like Jenny and the captain, Mara and Dora had apparently seen what happened to the little goats, too. The girls were scampering across the upper fields laying wire to discourage any more wild creatures from descending the hills into the battlegrounds.

There was no letup. The dreadful sounds from relentless machine guns, the deafening movements of the tanks, the occasional cries of pain, and the yelling of more orders to kill continued.

Jenny watched as the Krishna-lanians continued

to avoid trouble, using their deflectors. If they were caught unawares and couldn't move their image fast enough, they used a form of judo with hand grips that rendered their attackers unconscious. Jenny hadn't seen this tactic before.

It was ugly and awful. Jenny's sobs never stopped. Nor did her hands and feet as she ran to set up her equipment. In front of her was a machine gun propped against a log; at her side was the rifle as a backup.

She would never know whether she'd have fired or not.

She saw, across the right field, a tall, angular figure spin high into the air—as if something had caught his shoulder at an angle—and go down.

"Captain!" Jenny shouted.

She was small, but she was strong. Today, she was even stronger with fury at this barbaric army invading the beautiful, peaceful city of Krishna-la, and attacking her friends so mercilessly.

As Jenny raced across the field, she knocked away everything in her path—men, guns, supplies, and anything else that lay between her and the captain.

Captain Fisher wasn't quite dead. Jenny could see that his shoulder had been dislocated, and his shrapnel wounds were bleeding badly.

"He's unconscious," Jenny said, "thank goodness. There aren't too many things more painful than a dislocated shoulder." She was speaking to Laurie, who was there the minute she saw what had happened.

"You're all right?" asked Jenny.

Laurie nodded. "I'm all right," she said grimly. "But I never want to hear another word about the joys of the future."

"But it isn't Krishna-la that's causing the trouble," said Jenny. While she was talking, she was positioning the captain's arm the way she'd seen her father do it. "Those soldiers are ours. They're from Earth."

"So how come no one from here is stopping them? How come Mike's been—killed—and the captain nearly, and heaven only knows where Joe is," said Laurie. "With all their other powers, you'd think—"

But there wasn't much time to think. Fighting broke out not far from where Jenny and Laurie were taking care of the captain.

"Can I help?" The welcome voice was that of Damon Lanza.

"I'm glad you're here," said Jenny. "I need help with the captain's shoulder."

Damon Lanza and Jenny repositioned the captain's shoulder joint, and bound his arm in a tight sling with a strip from the bottom of Jenny's night-gown. The pain from this first-aid procedure would have been awful enough to knock anyone out. It was a blessing that the captain was already unconscious. The three carried him to the edge of the forest, away from the action.

"Anyone seen Joe Scott?" Jenny asked. She mopped her face, perspiring from the exertion.

Damon Lanza nodded. "Last I saw, he was way on the other side of the battlefield beyond those rocks. He was doing an amazing job of holding off the tallest human creature I've ever seen. He had dark brown skin and was exceptionally agile, grace-ful, and fast. Looked royal to me."

"The Masai warrior," said Jenny. "You're right, the Masai have royal blood, and they are fast and graceful warriors. But what is one doing here in Krishna-la? Something is truly strange here, Laurie, truly strange."

"I don't want to say something as fascinating as 'no kidding,' Jen, but no kidding!" answered Laurie.

Jenny paused on the sidelines of the battlefield for a few moments to let her rage subside, to think and to figure a solution to these mysterious happenings.

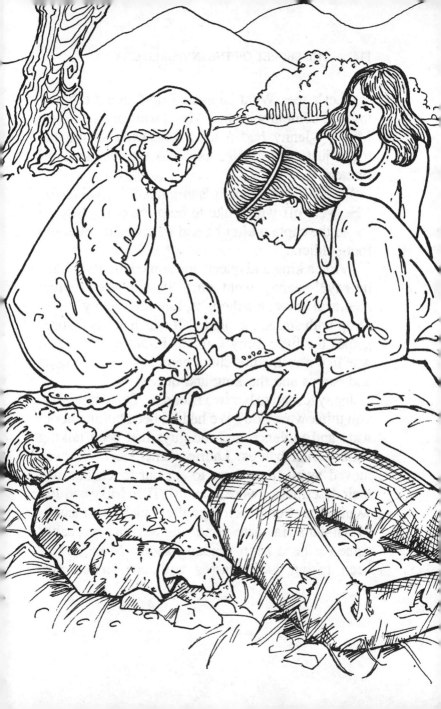

"Let's see. What happened first? Joe did hand-to-hand combat with that Masai warrior first. Then Mike"—Jenny had a hard time even saying his name just yet—"Mike ran into the two samurai fighters."

"Wasn't it the captain's turn next?" said Laurie. "He went off with Mike to help Joe out. Then we found the captain after he had been beaten by some foot-soldiers."

"And a king and queen and some knights, didn't he say?" Jenny went on. "It was like a small medieval army, we thought, Laurie." Jenny's eyes lit up with sudden insight. "It was like his favorite game, the little army Captain Fisher described. It was like a miniature chess game, with the knights and pawns and the king and queen."

Jenny turned to her two friends. "Do you see? Do you think what I do? We had all been talking about wars and violence and the guys had been talking about actual battles, Laurie, remember? We even moved away from them to eat our lunch because their descriptions were so awful. Then Mike and Joe went off to stretch their legs after lunch. Joe meets a Masai—his favorite kind of warrior, probably someone he'd been thinking about. Mike, who's been taking judo classes with Joe, meets two samurai, probably the kind of fighters he'd been thinking about. And what does the captain think about all the time these days? Chessmen and the battle of the chessboard.''

"That's right,'' said Laurie, admiring the logic of her friend.

"And where are we?'' said Jenny. "In a space city where whatever you think of, whatever is in your mind, can instantly come alive, from a clothes boutique to a theater with your own productions to a mountain full of one's favorite creatures to . . .''

Jenny was suddenly and absolutely quiet.

Then, in another moment, she shouted, waving her arms and running right out into the thick of the battle, "Stop! Everybody stop!''

"She's gone mad,'' Laurie cried to Damon Lanza. "Catch her, please, Damon Lanza. Jenny's gone mad!''

CHAPTER 14

Mike Returns

Jenny knew what was the matter. So why couldn't she stop it? The whole thing, the whole explanation for all this violence—for the fights, for the infantry and tanks, the rifles, machine guns—was all clear in her mind. Since her mind was clear about it all, her mind ought to be able to stop it all. Only it wasn't stopping. The shots continued to strafe the air.

"Concentrate harder," she commanded herself. "Make this awful war go away in your mind, and it will go away from this battlefield."

To help herself concentrate, Jenny squeezed her eyes shut and held her head with her hands as if to hold her thoughts together.

"Jenny! Jenny, they're shooting at you. Come back out of there." Jenny could hear Laurie's voice over the whine of the bullets.

"Jenny, use your image deflector. I'm on my way." Now it was Damon Lanza's voice.

But Jenny didn't want her friends to help, to add to the conflict. She wanted everybody to stop.

She happened to look up for a moment. What she saw high on the hill made her angry. There were Allessi and Allessa, standing tall in their silvery white robes, looking down at the battlefield.

They're doing nothing, thought Jenny angrily. They're just standing up there, looking down at us and doing nothing. While it was true that the Krishna-lanians who participated in the battle used their deflectors quickly and well, even they got caught once in a while by a bullet and went down. Jenny shook a fist up at the Heads of State.

"What am I doing?" she gasped. "Jenny, stop it," she ordered herself. She knew how angry thoughts only made things worse.

Then it happened. It had to, sooner or later. Jenny was right in the middle of the battlefield. She hadn't been able to stop the war with her mind as she'd hoped. And her feelings were growing angrier, not calmer, as she saw her Krishna-lanian friends go down, as she remembered the captain's pain, and as she remembered, most of all, always, every moment, the loss of her Mike.

"Jenny, get down!" Laurie was screaming now, fighting her way through the battlefield toward her friend.

It was too late.

A rifle bullet tore into Jenny's leg. The pain was bad. So were the disconnected thoughts that she might not ever run . . . or play tennis . . . or dance again. Whoever described war as heroic? It was so painful . . . so degrading . . . an inhuman waste.

Then as Jenny fell under the crush of a small mob of onrushing uniformed soldiers, she could feel all her anger give way to something else—a kind of sorrow for the human beings who had been hurting each other, their Earth, and its creatures, for so many thousands of years. It wasn't heroic, just useless, just sad.

As she slumped to the ground, Jenny murmured gently, "I do wish it would stop, all this meaningless revenge. What use is it? If I hurt you because you've hurt me, someone else will hurt someone for that hurt. Meaningless, meaningless," she kept on murmuring, as her heart filled with more and more sadness for the unintelligent ways of humankind.

She could feel herself still being trampled. Either she hurt so much she couldn't feel it anymore, or her body was in shock, or her mind had worked out some kind of defense system.

She was shot, trampled, bruised, and surrounded by such hordes of soldiers that her friends were

having a hard time getting to her. Jenny even wondered if it might be too late by the time they did get to
her.

Was this her last adventure?

Well, she'd had a good time, and a lot of love,
but—

"I'll miss it," Jenny went on murmuring to herself, her voice low and comforting as if she were her
own child. "But it's all right. I'm not angry at any of
it anymore, poor, sad, old world that won't learn
how to behave itself until everybody's hurting or
dead."

As her last drop of anger turned into this gentle
sadness, Jenny murmured just a few last words. "I
do wish it would stop. Oh, I do wish all the fighting
would stop."

Jenny's vanished anger was louder than a scream.

Suddenly, it was over, just simply over.

As if a movie reel had snapped and the lights
instantly had come on in a vast theater, the war was
over. The soldiers were gone from the fields between the forest and the hills and the city. The tanks
and rifles and machine guns were gone with them.

There wasn't even a trace of war. The sight and
smell of smoke had vanished. The outbreak of fires
had been quenched. Trampled grass was fresh and

green again. The Krishna-lanians who had defended themselves were standing about talking. Even the ones who had been wounded or killed had risen to join their fellows in conversational groups that either remained quietly where they were, or wandered off back toward the city.

Jenny tried to stand up. She was a little dizzy at first, but clearly, she was entirely mended. As she stood, she cried out.

"Captain, you're all right!" she called. His shoulder injury appeared healed, Jenny noticed as the captain strode toward her from the edge of the forest. On the way, he caught up with Laurie and Damon Lanza. From the rocks, Joe Scott appeared with Dora and Mara. No Masai warrior followed him now. The three of them waved and shouted at Jenny in greeting.

But there was still someone missing, someone Jenny longed to see with all her heart. But she knew she would never see him again. There was no anger now, only pity for the world and sadness. She was so glad the others were all safe and alive. She would try to comfort herself with that.

Then a figure appeared on the horizon. It stood there for a moment as if it were hovering on the rim of time. Then it came forward in fast, and, suddenly, to Jenny, recognizable strides. Jenny was off, leaping across the field, filled with such joy she could hardly breathe.

"Mike! It's you. It's really you!"

Mike's golden eyes glowed with pleasure at the sight of her, and his arms swept her tightly and held her close. After a time, he said, "Really, Jen, we must have a chat about what's fun and what's going too far. And what have you done to that night-gown?"

"Odd," said Jenny. "Flesh, grass, people are healed, and I still have a piece of my nightie missing from making a bandage for the captain."

"We've just come back from the dead," said Mike. "Why are we standing here discussing your nightgown?"

The two laughed just for the feel of it, held hands, and ran back toward the others.

By then, Allessi and Allessa had come down from the high place and joined them.

"What happened, Allessi?" said Jenny, straight to the point. "It was so sudden, so awful. Who could have started such a horrible war?"

Allessi's eyes held a dark twinkle.

"You did, Jenny, m'dear," he said. "You started the war."

CHAPTER 15

Peace at Last

"How is that possible?" Jenny demanded.

"That's what I want to know," said Laurie. "I mean no disrespect, sir, but you haven't known Jenny as long as we have. Mike and Joe and Jenny and I have been close since the second grade. We've spent a lot of that time teasing her unmercifully about her inability to stop saving the world."

"Laurie's right, Allessi," said Mike. His hand ruffled Jenny's short mop of blond hair and he smiled down at her bright, intense eyes. "Our Jenny Dean once stopped a Memorial Day Parade down Elm Street because some frogs had hopped too far from Bitterblue Forest. Everything came to a halt until the frogs had crossed Elm Street. I mean, sir, she can be a royal pain in the neck, if you know what I'm saying, but she could never start a war."

The tinkling glass sound of Allessa's laughter filled the air.

"Nevertheless," she seconded her husband's statement, "Jenny did start the war. Begin with the premise that what Jenny discovered is true. In Krishna-la, whatever the mind can think of, whatever is in the mind, can happen."

Captain Fisher, who had been quiet until then, thinking things through logically as usual, with as little emotional interference as possible, spoke softly to Jenny.

"We've reasoned things out together before, Jenny," he said. "We must reason this through *without* either emotion or preconceptions such as 'Jenny saves frogs and other creatures' or 'Jenny is the kindest person we all know.' Not that those things aren't true, but they may cover up facts we need to understand all this. The statement that you started the war is difficult enough to understand, given your dedication to nonviolence. But such a dedication means giving attention to violence and not acting upon it. We all get angry, though, sometimes."

Jenny, who had been even quieter than the captain for a few minutes, was suddenly startled out of her thought process. "Anger—that's the word, Captain. Now I understand. Yes, of course, everybody. I certainly did start this war."

"Would you like to explain that piece of nonsense?" said Joe Scott, still unwilling to believe that Jenny Dean was the antagonist in this drama, the bad guy in the play, so to speak.

As they were talking all this through, Allessa had been leading, pushing, guiding an elbow here, leaning against an arm there, until she had got them all started back to the Palace of the Winds.

Almost without their knowing it, all ten, Jenny and her friends and the Heads of State with their three progeny, were soon sitting over tea and bran cakes and honey around the round, glass table in the main hall of the crystal palace.

Jenny nodded and began. "In the middle of the battle, I understood suddenly that just as any mind probe could tell Laurie loved clothes, or Joe the theater, or the captain his music and chess, any mind probe could equally tell our negative stuff. Not only our pleasures, but our angers and fears could be satisfied, also."

Jenny looked to Allessi for confirmation as she spoke. He smiled, and nodded.

Jenny went on. "So what I figured was that at lunch, the men had all been talking of fighting and wars. Very quickly, each was granted precisely what was on his mind—Joe, a Masai warrior, Mike,

two samurai to test his new judo maneuvers on, and the captain, actual chessmen making strategic moves."

"Good, so far," said Allessi, sipping his hot tea and spreading honey on a bran cake. He seemed to be enjoying Jenny's recital.

"The business of the war had me puzzled," said Jenny. "I couldn't understand where so *much* violence had come from."

Then she blushed. Admission came hard. But Jenny knew she'd feel better with the truth out. "I have such an image of myself sometimes as just too saintly for words. The whole thing escaped me until just a little while ago," she said. "But the truth is, I was so angry because Joe got hurt. Then when Mike and the captain were also hurt, I was even angrier. It was the violence of my anger at Krishna-la and the hurting of my friends that must have produced in the back of my mind enough energy to create an entire infantry battalion complete with its own tank force. Then, of course, when the army materialized and even more people were hurt—to say nothing of Mike's, of Mike's seeming to die—I was in a blaze. Gone were all the discussions of how violence doesn't end as long as it's met with more violence. Part of me cared, of course. And ordinarily I wouldn't have gone looking for guns myself. But obviously part of me is still a barbarian, and I must have brought that whole army from my mind right onto the fields of Krishna-la.''

"True, exactly," said Allessi.

''But if it was all an illusion, why was the pain so real, why was the army so cruel?'' said Mike.

"Once you dream up fighters and killers, you can't control the outcome," said Allessi. "Even in an illusion, the pain is very real. On Krishna-la, we just happen to know well the difference between illusion and reality. So even if an illusion hurts us, we'd know it was just an entertainment.''

"Entertainment?" said Joe in protest.

Allessi nodded. "Just so. The minds of Mike and Joe and Captain Fisher seemed entertained at the thought of battles with warriors and knights and samurai. So we simply created such an entertainment for them. Jenny's mind seemed to require a wholesale conflict to satisfy her mood. So we created an entire war for her.''

Jenny laughed ruefully, thoroughly embarrassed. "I'm going to think out more carefully what I think I want from now on," she said. "This time what I got was awful." Jenny turned to the captain. "You know, it was when you used the word 'anger' I understood why the battle ended when it did and not before.''

"Tell," said Laurie, who had been wondering about that herself.

"Well," said Jenny, "as long as I was running around angrily shouting at everyone to stop being angry, my anger at the fighting must have just gone on feeding the war. When my own angry feelings left, so did the army produced by those feelings."

"Just like that," said Laurie admiringly.

"Just like that," said Jenny. "But now that I've answered some questions, Allessi, would you?"

"I think so," said Allessi.

"How come guards escorted me out from your underground places where your equipment is stored?" said Jenny. She still had lingering suspicions that they were trying to hide something.

"That's easy," said Allessi. "We try to keep any new technology hidden from Earth people. We're not the only self-contained artificial world voyaging through the universe, you know. We've all agreed to be careful on this point. Sometimes, without your knowing it, civilizations like our Krishna-la have left tools or new techniques in Earth minds or in Earth laboratories—you know, like the story of your tooth fairy leaving quarters under pillows for you to find in the morning. But humans still use tools and technology for aggression, for competing with each other instead of getting along with each other. So we try to let you find out as little as possible whenever possible.''

Jenny laughed. ''And I thought you were hiding special machinery to conquer Earth.''

Damon Lanza, Dora, and Mara found that funny. ''Why in the name of the cosmos should we want to do that?'' said Damon Lanza.

''I even thought you might want to kidnap the five of us,'' said Jenny.

''Well, you're not really advanced enough for us to find you either instructive or entertaining yet,'' said Allessi. ''But we have great hopes for you. We're grateful as always for the opportunity to study Earth, and to you all, in particular, for being gracious enough to let us study your minds. But much as we've come to love you all, we'll bid you farewell for another thousand years or so.''

''Finish your tea, dear,'' said Allessa, patting Jenny's hand. ''Just a little more honey on the bran cake, Michael? Joe, Laurie, another cake? Captain Fisher, more tea?''

''Thank you, no,'' said the captain, his deep, polite voice resonating from the crystal heights of the Palace of the Winds.

Then—and Jenny only remembered this afterwards, a few moments later—there was that odd sensation of emotional and mental blackout.

When the five friends blinked their eyes and came out of that blackout, the Valley of the Blue Stars was gone, simply gone. The five were standing alone in the absolute emptiness of the raw, gray, windswept Kansas plains on a late November afternoon.

After a few minutes of quiet, Jenny said in a small voice, "Did all that happen?"

"Did all *what* happen?" said the others, to tease.

"Funny," said Jenny. "Fu-unny!"

An hour's walk, and they were all back at the farmhouse. Oddly, Aunt Sally greeted them as if there wasn't anything so very surprising about two of them disappearing for such an extended time without a word, and five people returning.

"Dessert and coffee?" Aunt Sally said hospitably, and Uncle John pulled out chairs around the cozy kitchen table.

"How long does it seem to you we've been gone, Aunt Sally?" Jenny asked.

"Just today for a few hours," said Aunt Sally, "and thank goodness for it. I needed this whole Friday to clear up after yesterday's Thanksgiving dinner."

"Amazing," said Jenny. "They kept their time

separate entirely from ours on Earth. We were only gone a day.''

"Who's amazing?'' said Jenny's cousin Martha. "Who kept separate time? And how did Laurie and Joe and the captain get here so fast?''

Over three kinds of pie and coffee, they all told the story of Allessi and Allessa, of the Palace of the Winds and the Valley of the Blue Stars, of theaters and computer libraries and space pods, and of an armed battle against a city of crystal from an Andromeda galaxy billions of parsecs in space from the Milky Way.

"I don't think I believe a word of it,'' said Uncle John after the story was told.

"I wonder how long we'll believe it ourselves,'' said the captain.

"Captain,'' said Jenny softly. "You've always told me you don't have to believe in a fact. A fact is there, like a tree, whether you believe in it or not.''

The captain grew thoughtful. After a few moments, he drew something from his pocket, as if he had just remembered it was there. What he pulled from his pocket, Jenny recognized instantly and with joy. It was proof, if proof was needed. It was the one bit of the war that hadn't fixed itself. It was the torn strip of nightgown with which Jenny had bound the captain's wound.

Suddenly, she felt a sense of loss. Krishna-la was gone.

Yet always, the whispering of the universe, the trillions of stars, of alien suns, and the sound of laughter that tinkled like crystal would remain with her.

The captain replaced the piece of torn cloth affectionately in his pocket. Then seriously he said, "And speaking of facts, Jenny, as soon as we get back to Winter Falls, I want you to meet a behavioral scientist at the university. He's a friend of mine, whose latest invention to explore human behavior—past and present—is some sort of time warp screen."

"Oh no, Captain," said Laurie. "If I know Jenny, she'll be looking for ghosts in that time warp machine."

But Jenny's mind still wasn't quite ready for the past or even the present yet. Her mind was still partly millions of years into the future, soaring somewhere into the vast reaches of starry space with her friends of Krishna-la.

About the Author

Dale Carlson is the author of more than thirty books for young people. Three of them, *The Mountain of Truth*, *The Human Apes*, and *Girls Are Equal Too* were ALA Notable Books; and her *Where's Your Head?* won a Christopher Award.

Ms. Carlson says that her daughter, Hannah, "edits all my current books, and also provides my favorite heroines. She is particularly the heroine of The Jenny Dean Science Fiction Mysteries." Her son, Danny, coauthored her book *The Shining Pool*.

Ms. Carlson lives in New York City.